# I SPY

## SUPER CHALLENGER!

## A BOOK OF PICTURE RIDDLES

Photographs by Walter Wick

Riddles by Jean Marzollo

Cartwheel
·B·O·O·K·S·®

SCHOLASTIC INC.

New York   Toronto   London   Auckland   Sydney
Mexico City   New Delhi   Hong Kong   Buenos Aires

For Zoë and Eva Morozko

———————

W.W.

For Ricky
and Zhao Hong

———————

J.M.

Book design by Carol Devine Carson

Text copyright © 1997 by Jean Marzollo.
Cover illustration copyright © 1997 by Walter Wick.
All rights reserved. Published by Scholastic Inc.
SCHOLASTIC, CARTWHEEL BOOKS, and associated logos
are trademarks and/or registered trademarks of Scholastic Inc.

"Tiny Toys," "Silhouettes," and "Toys in the Attic" from I Spy © 1992 by Walter Wick; "Stocking Stuffers"
from I Spy Christmas © 1992 by Walter Wick; "Peanuts and Popcorn" from I Spy Fun House © 1993 by
Walter Wick; "Chain Reaction," "The Hidden Clue," and "A Whale of a Tale" from I Spy Mystery © 1993
by Walter Wick; "Flight of Fancy" and "City Blocks" from I Spy Fantasy © 1994 by Walter Wick; "Storybook
Theater" and "1, 2, 3" from I Spy School Days © 1995 by Walter Wick. All published by Scholastic Inc.

Library of Congress Cataloging-in-Publication Data is available.

ISBN-13: 978-0-439-91091-0
ISBN-10: 0-439-91091-9
12 11 10  9  7  6  5  4  3  2  1                    7  8  9  10  11  12/0

Printed in Singapore    46
This edition first printing, January 2007

# TABLE OF CONTENTS

Picture riddles fill this book;
Turn the pages! Take a look!

Use your mind, use your eye;
Read the riddles—play I SPY!

I spy a hydrant, an iron, a dart,
Two cowboy boots, a little glass heart;

Three birds, a bell, a beetle, a B,
A flame, and the Roman numeral III.

I spy three dogs, two cleaners for pipes,
A baby asleep, the Stars and Stripes;

Eyes with no face, a fireman's axe,
A trotting globe, and ten little jacks.

I spy two ladders, a duck and its twin,

A mousetrap, a sailor, a tiny clothespin;

A candle, a pipe, a watchband, a ball,
And a towering clown who will soon take a fall.

I spy a limo, a mouse, and a rock,

Two bows, a boat, a bee on a block;

A pencil, a golf tee, a church with a cross,
A jingle bell, and chocolate sauce.

I spy a penguin, a fine-tooth comb,

A zipper pull tab, and a little bird's home;

A cone from a sweetshop, a cone from a tree,
A bow tie, a tiger, a mouse, and a G.

I spy an apple, a house of bricks,
Four candy canes, and eight craft sticks;

An owl, a dragon, a cricket, a bee,
Musical notes, and the number three.

I spy two spurs, two dogs, two 8's,
Four red hands, four tops, two skates;

An off-on switch, a see-through trunk,
A paper clip, and a statue that shrunk.

I spy two snowmen, a walnut, a horn,
Paper-clip skates, an ear of corn;

A birthday candle, a brown-and-white dog,
A cricket, a soccer ball, and a hog.

I spy a bat, a balloon, a pail,

A box of potatoes, a horse's tail;

Two umbrellas, a little spare tire,
A baby bottle, ICE, and Fire.

I spy a nut, thirteen number nines,
Twenty-five spades, and three road signs;

Two pennies, two cacti, four arrows, a stork,
Six dominoes, five flags, and a fork.

I spy three clothespins, a fast-riding man,
A wooden heart, and a watering can;

A safety pin, a shiny blue hat,
A rat, a cat, a bat, and ALL THAT.

I spy a pumpkin, a white wooden chair,

Miss LAZYBONES, and a boot in the air;

A running dish, a hammer, a plane,
And hardest of all, a PAGE with a train.

# EXTRA CREDIT RIDDLES

## Find the Pictures That Go With These Riddles:

I spy an acorn, a telephone toy,

A key, and an angel drummer boy.

I spy a rainbow, a bird that is blue,

Ballet slippers, and binoculars, too.

I spy a blue boot, a small fish with fins,

A jump rope, and ten white bowling pins.

I spy a sea horse, teeth, and a V,

A domino, and a wooden D.

I spy a flag and a small puzzle piece,

Three barrels, two hens, and worn-out fleece.

I spy a peeking giraffe, a truck,

Six red shoes, and a little blue duck.

I spy a knight, four pigs' tails,

Two scary wolves, and two little pails.

I spy a taxi, a woman with a cane,

A domino, eight black dots near a plane.

I spy a horseshoe, a broom, four B's,

OIL, eight crab legs, and three little trees.

I spy a strainer, the point of a pen,

A wrench, a zebra, and three sportsmen.

I spy three mice, a tortoise, a hare,

An itchy colt, and a climbing bear.

I spy a sandal, a game-board shoe,

A grand piano, and Pegasus, too.

# About the Creators of *I Spy*

**Jean Marzollo** has written many award-winning children's books, including twelve I Spy Books, seven I Spy Little Books, and eleven I Spy Readers. She has also written *I Love You: A Rebus Poem*, illustrated by Suse MacDonald; *I Am Planet Earth*, illustrated by Judith Moffatt; *Happy Birthday, Martin Luther King*, illustrated by Brian Pinkney; *Thanksgiving Cats*, illustrated by Hans Wilhelm; *Shanna's Princess Show* and *Shanna's Doctor Show*, illustrated by Shane Evans; *Pretend You're a Cat*, illustrated by Jerry Pinkney; *Mama Mama*, illustrated by Laura Regan; *Home Sweet Home*, illustrated by Ashley Wolff; *Soccer Sam*, illustrated by Blanche Sims; and *Close Your Eyes*, illustrated by Susan Jeffers. Most recently she has written and illustrated a highly acclaimed series of Bible stories for young children. For nineteen years, Jean Marzollo and Carol Carson produced Scholastic's kindergarten magazine, *Let's Find Out*. Ms. Marzollo holds a masters degree from the Harvard Graduate School of Education. She is the 2000 recipient of the Rip Van Winkle Award presented by the School Library Media Specialists of Southeastern New York. She lives with her husband, Claudio, in New York State's Hudson Valley.

**Walter Wick** is the photographer of the I Spy Books. He is the author and photographer of *A Drop of Water: A Book of Science and Wonder*, which won the *Boston Globe/Horn Book* Award for Nonfiction, was named a Notable Children's Book by the American Library Association, and was selected as an Orbis Pictus Honor Book and a CBC/NSTA Outstanding Science Trade Book for Children. *Walter Wick's Optical Tricks*, a book of photographic illusions, was named a Best Illustrated Children's Book by the *New York Times* Book Review, was recognized as a Notable Children's Book by the American Library Association, and received many awards, including the Platinum Award from the Oppenheim Toy Portfolio, a Young Reader's Award from *Scientific American*, a *Bulletin* Blue Ribbon, and a Parent's Choice Silver Honor. His most recent series, Can You See What I See?, has appeared on the *New York Times* Bestseller List. Mr. Wick has invented photographic games for *Games Magazine* and photographed covers for books and magazines, including *Newsweek*, *Discover*, and *Psychology Today*. A graduate of Paier College of Art, Mr. Wick lives with his wife, Linda, in Connecticut.

**Carol Devine Carson**, the book designer for the I Spy series, is art director for a major publishing house in New York City.

# Write Your Own Picture Riddles

There are many more hidden objects and many more possibilities for riddles in this book. Write some rhyming picture riddles yourself, and try them out with friends.

## The Story of *I Spy Super Challenger!*

For years children who have found every single thing in every single *I Spy* Book have begged for a harder book to challenge their visual and mental skills. Consequently, Walter Wick and Jean Marzollo selected from previous *I Spy* Books the hardest pictures — the ones with the most objects. Jean Marzollo then asked children in second and third grade to tell her which objects were the most difficult to find. With their comments and eager spirit in mind, she wrote brand-new rhyming riddles. Warning to grown-ups: if this book is too hard for you, enlist some children to help.

### Acknowledgments

We'd like to thank the many children and their teachers who tested these riddles for us: William, Isaac, Tommi Ann, Alessandra, Rebecca, Geoffrey, Chad, Ian, Tom, Amanda, Robbie, Jeff, Caitlin, Laila, Owen, and Mrs. Donna Norkeliunas; Kerry, Dani, Ryan, David, Sasha, Sam, Ray, Matt W., Lucas, Maike, Jo, Desi, Lana, Kim, Erica, Marty, Billy, Sophie, Rachael, Matt H., Jasen, Matt A., and Ms. Brennan; Jordan, Lee, Justine, Erin, Ryan, Adrienne, Brandon, Katie, Hannah, and Greyson. We'd also like to thank David Marzollo for his outstanding creative input.

Jean Marzollo and Walter Wick

I Spy Books for All Ages:
I SPY: A BOOK OF PICTURE RIDDLES
I SPY CHRISTMAS
I SPY EXTREME CHALLENGER!
I SPY FANTASY
I SPY FUN HOUSE
I SPY GOLD CHALLENGER!
I SPY MYSTERY
I SPY SCHOOL DAYS
I SPY SPOOKY NIGHT
I SPY SUPER CHALLENGER!
I SPY TREASURE HUNT
I SPY ULTIMATE CHALLENGER!
I SPY YEAR-ROUND CHALLENGER!

I Spy Books for New Readers:
I SPY A BALLOON
I SPY A BUTTERFLY
I SPY A CANDY CANE
I SPY A DINOSAUR'S EYE
I SPY FUNNY TEETH
I SPY LIGHTNING IN THE SKY
I SPY A PENGUIN
I SPY A PUMPKIN
I SPY SANTA CLAUS
I SPY A SCARY MONSTER
I SPY A SCHOOL BUS

And I Spy Books for the Youngest Child:
I SPY LITTLE ANIMALS
I SPY LITTLE BOOK
I SPY LITTLE BUNNIES
I SPY LITTLE CHRISTMAS
I SPY LITTLE LEARNING BOX
I SPY LITTLE LETTERS
I SPY LITTLE NUMBERS
I SPY LITTLE WHEELS

Also available:
I SPY CHALLENGER! FOR GAME BOY ADVANCE
I SPY JUNIOR: PUPPET PLAYHOUSE CD-ROM
I SPY JUNIOR CD-ROM
I SPY SCHOOL DAYS CD-ROM
I SPY SPOOKY MANSION CD-ROM
I SPY TREASURE HUNT CD-ROM